The King's Flower

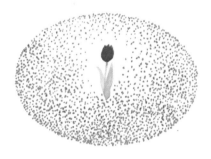

Library of Congress Cataloging in Publication Data

Anno, Mitsumasa, 1926–
  The King's Flower.

SUMMARY: A king discovers that bigger is not always better.
  [1. Size and shape—Fiction]   I. Title.
PZ7.A5875Ki   1978   [E]   78-9596
ISBN 0-529-05458-2
ISBN 0-529-05459-0 lib. bdg.

MITSUMASA ANNO
The King's Flower

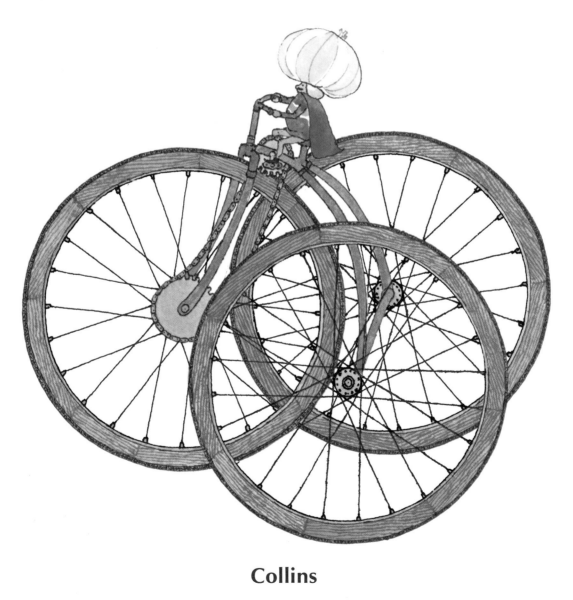

Collins

New York and Cleveland

There was once a King who had to have everything bigger and better than anyone else. He lived in a very big castle and he wore such a very big crown that it was actually rather uncomfortable. He slept in an enormous bed, so high he had to use a ladder to get in and out of it. The King's toothbrush was so big it took two men just to carry it.

When the big clock
chimed in the kitchen the noise
was quite deafening. It was the signal
to start preparing the King's big breakfast.

The King's knife and fork were so big that they had to be hung from the ceiling with ropes and pulleys and he found it very difficult to use them. Soon, of course, the King was hungry.

9

The food he liked best of all was choco-late, so he sent his servants out to fetch some. They brought him the biggest bar of chocolate ever seen, too big even to get through the castle gate. So the King had to go outside to nibble a bit from the end of it.

"How delicious," he said. "This is the biggest and best chocolate bar ever. Just right for a man of my importance." And he ate some more, and some more, until . . .

"Help! Call the dentist. My tooth hurts most dreadfully," cried the King.

"Only the biggest of everything for the King," remembered the dentist. So he ordered the blacksmiths to make a gigantic pair of pincers to pull out the royal tooth.

The King was just a little uneasy when he saw the huge pincers and again when the dentist tied him down in his chair. But everyone pushed or pulled and at last out came the tiny bad tooth and the King's enormous toothache was over.

The next day the King ordered his servants to take the pincers away.

"Turn them into a birdcage or something," he commanded, for that is what their shape reminded him of.

It was a beautifully big birdcage but the spaces between the bars were so wide that the birds he put inside the cage flew out again. "What a disappointment," said the King.

One day not long after, however, a great eagle flew over the castle trying to catch some of the little birds. Swiftly they flew back into the new cage and were quite safe, for the eagle could not get through the bars. The King was very pleased.

"I knew biggest was best," he said.

Then the King had another idea and he commanded his servants to build the biggest flower-pot ever made and to fill it with tons of earth. A single tulip bulb was planted in the middle.

"In such a big flower-pot, this one tulip cannot fail to be the biggest and best in all the world," said the King.

While he waited for the tulip to grow, the King ordered that the hole from where the earth had been taken should be made into a pond for fishing. But the first fishing rod that was brought to him was much too small.

"I must have a bigger line," he ordered. "I want to catch the biggest fish in all the world."

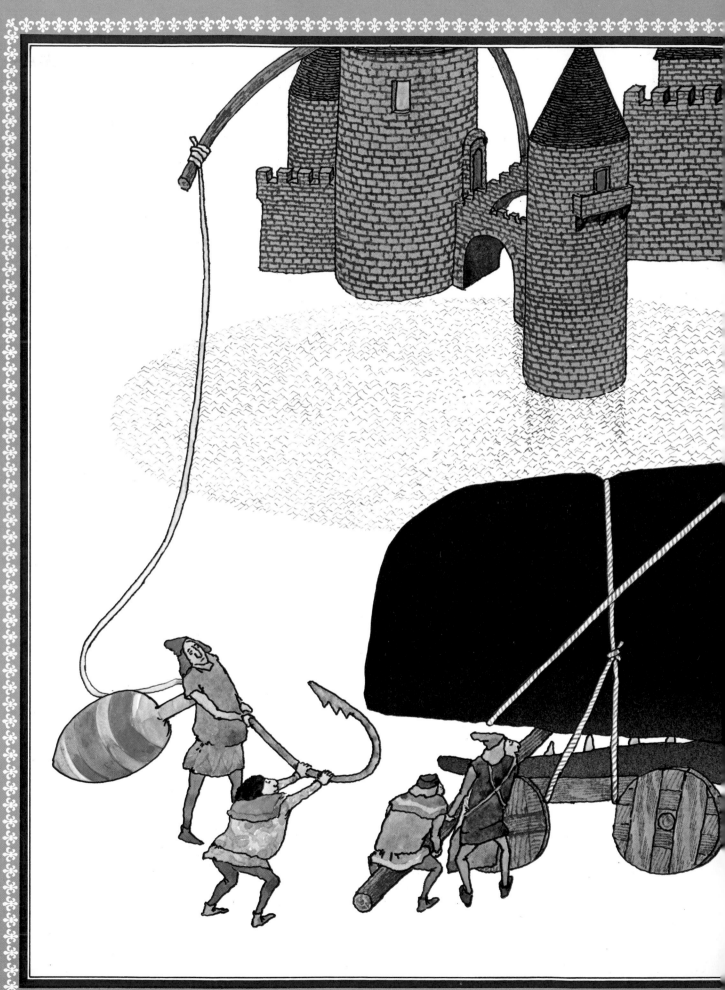

The servants knew that the King would not let them rest until he had caught the biggest fish, so they brought in a whale and attached it to the hook. The King was very pleased with his catch but the fish was too heavy for him to lift out of the water and he had to let it go.

Every morning the King climbed up into the big flower-pot to see if the tulip was growing, but there was no sign of it. The King's gardener comforted him.

"The biggest and best flower in all the world is bound to take longer to grow than an ordinary flower," he said.

At last, one spring day, when the King peered over the edge of the pot, there it was! A red tulip blossomed serenely in the middle of the enormous flower-pot. The King looked at it for a long time. It was not big. It was small — but it was very beautiful.

"Perhaps biggest is not best after all," said the King, wondering at the work of nature. "Not even I could make the biggest flower in all the world. And perhaps that is just as well."

Anno's Afterword

One day, when I was looking at a gas storage tank, I wondered what it would be like if there was a coffee cup as large as one of these big containers. I imagined myself climbing up a tall ladder and creeping along the edge on my hands and knees, lapping up the coffee, and I felt almost dizzy. It gives me endless pleasure just imagining huge things—a pencil as large as a telegraph pole, a playground slide as high as a mountain, and a shoe so enormous that I could lie down in it. But could there ever be a tulip as large as an umbrella? The Egyptian kings built the great tombs, the Pyramids, but even the most powerful human beings cannot produce life. We must be content, and recognize that each flower, each worm, is something natural and indispensable.

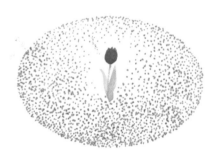

Photo: Ingrid Parge

About the Author

Mitsumasa Anno has long been acknowledged as one of Japan's leading illustrators and book designers. He was born in 1926 in Tsuwana, a small historic town in the western part of Japan, and graduated from the Yamagushi Teacher Training College. He worked as a primary school teacher for a time before starting his career as an artist. Mr Anno now lives in Tokyo with his wife and two daughters. He has received much acclaim for three earlier picture books: **Anno's Alphabet**, **Anno's Counting Book**, and **Anno's Journey**, and he has several more books in preparation.